Dear Parent:
Your child's love of reading starts here!

Every child learns to read in a different way and at his or her own speed. Some go back and forth between reading levels and read favorite books again and again. Others read through each level in order. You can help your young reader improve and become more confident by encouraging his or her own interests and abilities. From books your child reads with you to the first books he or she reads alone, there are I Can Read Books for every stage of reading:

SHARED READING
Basic language, word repetition, and whimsical illustrations, ideal for sharing with your emergent reader

BEGINNING READING
Short sentences, familiar words, and simple concepts for children eager to read on their own

READING WITH HELP
Engaging stories, longer sentences, and language play for developing readers

READING ALONE
Complex plots, challenging vocabulary, and high-interest topics for the independent reader

ADVANCED READING
Short paragraphs, chapters, and exciting themes for the perfect bridge to chapter books

I Can Read Books have introduced children to the joy of reading since 1957. Featuring award-winning authors and illustrators and a fabulous cast of beloved characters, I Can Read Books set the standard for beginning readers.

A lifetime of discovery begins with the magical words "I Can Read!"

Visit www.icanread.com for information
on enriching your child's reading experience.

Flat Stanley and the Firehouse. Text copyright © 2011 by the Trust u/w/o Richard C. Brown a/k/a Jeff Brown f/b/o Duncan Brown. Illustrations by Macky Pamintuan, copyright © 2011 by HarperCollins Publishers. All rights reserved. Manufactured in China. No part of this book may be used or reproduced in any manner whatsoever without written permission except in the case of brief quotations embodied in critical articles and reviews. For information address HarperCollins Children's Books, a division of HarperCollins Publishers, 10 East 53rd Street, New York, NY 10022.
www.icanread.com

Library of Congress catalog card number: 2010925409
ISBN 978-0-06-143006-0 (trade bdg.) — ISBN 978-0-06-143009-1 (pbk.)

Typography by Sean Boggs

11 12 13 14 15 SCP 10 9 8 7 6 5 4 3 2 1 ❖ First Edition

I Can Read!™

READING
2
WITH HELP

FLAT STANLEY
and the Firehouse

created by Jeff Brown
written by Lori Haskins Houran
pictures by Macky Pamintuan

HARPER
An Imprint of HarperCollinsPublishers

Stanley Lambchop lived

with his mother,

his father,

and his little brother, Arthur.

Stanley was four feet tall,

about a foot wide,

and half an inch thick.

He had been flat ever since

a bulletin board fell on him.

Stanley's family found it handy
having a flat boy at home,
and Stanley didn't mind helping out.
Stanley held tools for his father
while Mr. Lambchop repaired the car.

Stanley helped Arthur
practice his backflips.

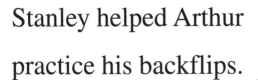

Stanley gave Mrs. Lambchop
a perfect place to roll out piecrust,
except when he
felt ticklish.

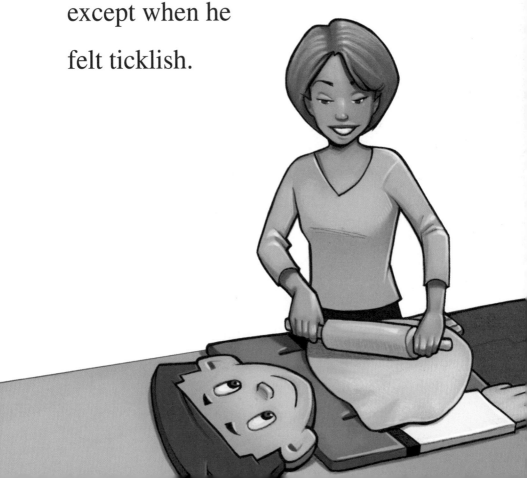

Stanley made a good stencil, too.

"Hold still," said Arthur.

Stanley held his breath
as Arthur traced him carefully.

Children all over the city
were entering a poster contest
for Fire Safety Month.

"I hope we win the trip
to the firehouse!" said Arthur.
"Me, too," said Stanley.
"I have always wanted
to slide down the pole."

The next Monday, a letter arrived.

"Hey, guess what?" shouted Arthur.

"Hay is for horses,"

Mrs. Lambchop said.

"Try to remember that, dear."

"Sorry," said Arthur. "Guess what?
Our poster won the contest.
We're going to the firehouse
on Saturday!"
Mrs. Lambchop clapped.
"I knew you boys had my talent
for art," she said proudly.

Stanley and Arthur practiced

fire drills all week long.

Arthur crawled around the house

on his hands and knees.

Stanley did the Stop, Drop, and Roll.

(Mostly the Roll.)

At last, Saturday came.

The Lambchops drove to the firehouse.

"Welcome!" bellowed Chief Abbot.

A puppy bounced at his feet.

"ARF ARF ARF ARF ARF!"

"Don't mind Spark," said the chief.

"He's still in training!"

Chief Abbot led the Lambchops
through the firehouse kitchen.
"We firefighters cook up
some tasty meals," he said.
Mr. Lambchop got out his camera.
He took a picture of a pot of chili.

Everyone went on to the bunk room.

"Very nice," said Mrs. Lambchop.

"Can I see the trucks?" said Arthur.

"Of course!" said Chief Abbot.

He led everyone down to the garage.

Stanley was disappointed.

He had wanted to get there by pole.

Boots and pants lay on the floor.

"Oh my," said Mrs. Lambchop.

"I could tidy up if you'd like."

Chief Abbot laughed.

"We leave these out so we can jump

into them in an emergency," he said.

"Neat!" said Stanley.

Chief Abbot pointed to

the ladder truck.

"Climb on up if you like."

"Wow!" said Arthur.

The boys scrambled onto the truck.

Spark was right behind them.

Suddenly, the alarm bell rang.

"Chief, Code 9 on Oak Street,"

called a firefighter.

The chief turned to the Lambchops.

"How would you folks like

to come along on a rescue?"

"A rescue? Will it be safe?"

asked Mr. Lambchop.

"You bet!" said Chief Abbot.

"Code 9 means a cat up a tree.

Probably Furball again."

Mr. Lambchop looked at his wife.

She gave a little nod.

"YES!" yelled Stanley and Arthur.

"Stanley, turn on the siren!

Arthur, hit the lights!"

shouted Chief Abbot.

"My goodness, is that necessary?"

asked Mrs. Lambchop.

"No," said Chief Abbot.

"It's just more fun this way!"

The truck raced out of the station.

Soon, it pulled up to a tall tree.

A tiny cat shivered at the top.

"She's pretty high up this time,"

said Chief Abbot.

Spark panted at the chief's feet.

"All right. Let's get her down."

Two firefighters raised the ladder.

The Lambchops moved out of the way.

Chief Abbot climbed until
Furball was just a few feet away.
"Good kitty," he said,
stretching out his hands.
"Come here, Furball."

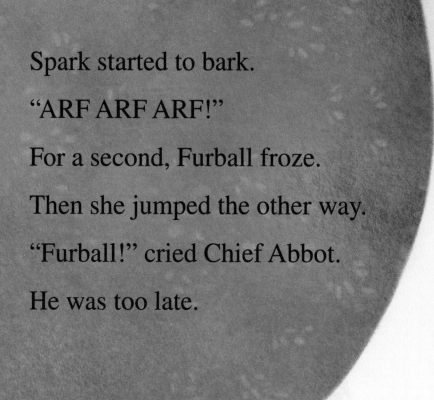

Spark started to bark.

"ARF ARF ARF!"

For a second, Furball froze.

Then she jumped the other way.

"Furball!" cried Chief Abbot.

He was too late.

Furball was heading

for the ground!

The Lambchops looked up.

Their mouths were open

in surprise.

All at once, Stanley threw

himself onto the grass.

"Grab my hands!"

he told his mother.

Mrs. Lambchop grabbed his hands.

"Grab my feet!" he told Arthur.

But Arthur didn't move.

"HEY!" shouted Mrs. Lambchop
at the top of her lungs.
"GRAB HIS FEET!"
Arthur blinked.
He grabbed Stanley's feet.

"Stretch!" cried Stanley.

Arthur and Mrs. Lambchop

stretched Stanley between them.

They were not a second too soon.

BOING! "MEOW!"

Furball bounced on Stanley's belly,

then landed safely on the ground.

The firefighters started clapping.

Arthur and Mrs. Lambchop
stood Stanley back up.
Arthur looked at his mother.
"Hay is for horses," he said.
"Remember?"
Mrs. Lambchop grinned.

"Good work, Lambchops!"

said Chief Abbot, racing over.

"How can we ever thank you?"

"Well," said Stanley.

"There is one thing. . . ."